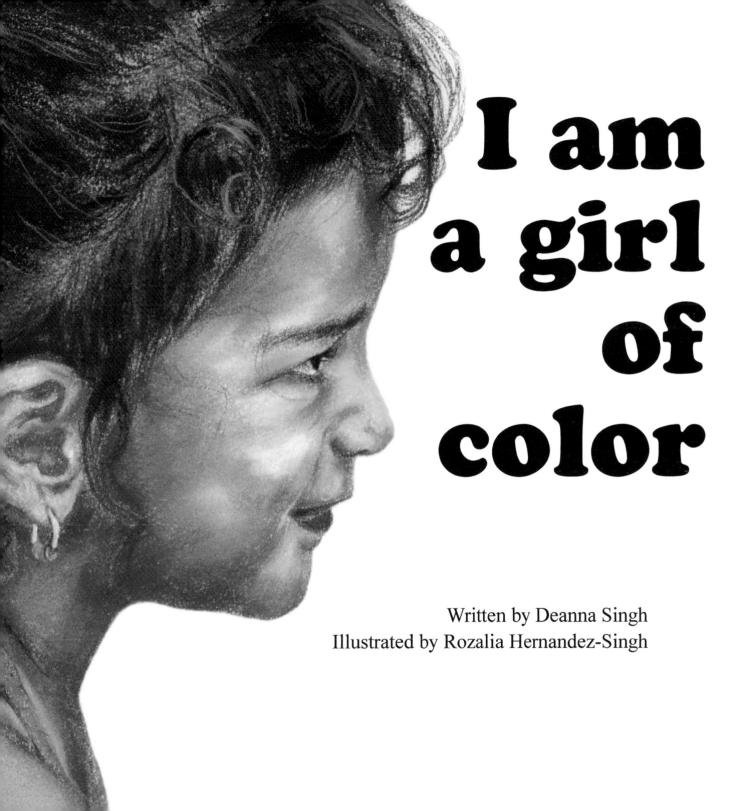

I am a girl of color

Written by Deanna Singh
Illustrated by Rozalia Hernandez-Singh

Presented by

Story to Tell Books

www.storytotellbooks.com

A Project of

*Flying*ELEPHANT

www.deannasingh.com

Published by Orange Hat Publishing
ISBN 978-0-692-91914-9

www.orangehatpublishing.com

To all of the girls who do not wait for permission
to claim their power.

When I look into a mirror,
I see BOLDNESS.

4

I do not let my fears hold me back from my dreams.

When I look into a mirror,
I see UNIQUENESS.
My face, my hair, my eyes are
perfect for me.

7

When I look into a mirror, I see BRILLIANCE.
I am full of great ideas.

When I look into a mirror, I see ARTISTRY.
I can make the world around me more beautiful.

11

When I look into a mirror, I see POSSIBILITY.

The world is a playground for my imagination.

13

When I look into a mirror,
I see MY ANCESTORS.

They paved a way for me to run towards my future.

When I look into a mirror,
I see A REFLECTION OF
GOD.

17

What do you see when you look at me?

I am Courageous.

I am Vivacious.

I am Inspiring.

I am Powerful.

23

I am Joyful.

I am Graceful.

25

I am a Girl of Color.

Draw an image of yourself!

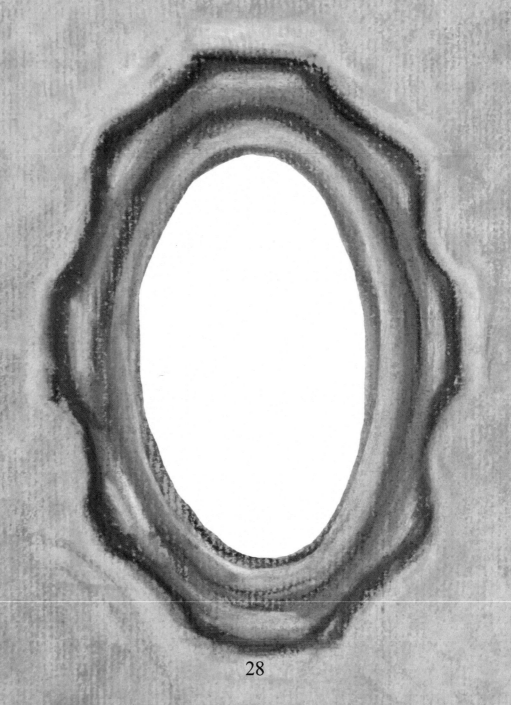

29

CPSIA information can be obtained at www.ICGtesting.com
Printed in the USA
LVIW01n1101061017
PP12723300001B/1